BAD RI[
AND OTH[

CURT TYLER

Copyright © 2024 Curt Tyler

All rights reserved.

Published by

facebook.com/curttylerfiction

curttylerfiction@gmail.com

For Maura, my love, who says she still likes my writing.

I DON'T DO DRUGS: I AM A DRUG!

A long queue to the dentist is the last thing you want to see when a toothache is killing you. Bad luck, I thought as I was squeezing my way through the swarms of dental casualties that had flooded the corridor, to reach the reception desk, which appeared at a distant horizon of the waiting room: a lighthouse for the crew of the ship lost at sea in a storm.

"Can I help you?" the receptionist asked.

I mumbled back that I needed a tooth to be removed. My words painted confusion on the receptionist's face so I opened my mouth and pointed at the culprit: the second molar on the left side of the upper jaw. Confusion turned into disgust, but the demonstration served its purpose. I filled in the form and collected my number: 666.

As I was squeezing my way back to the end of the queue, I thought of what constitutes consciousness: the electric impulses between neurons. I imagined I could see these tiny lightning bolts through the transparent heads of the people around me: buzzing cobwebs, floating above their necks.

I sat down and contemplated this carnival of dental atrocities. So much pain in such a small place.

I took out my mobile phone to occupy my mind with anything but the merciless inflammation devastating my jaw. As I scrolled through a social media page, a black-and-white photo of the surrealist painter, Dani Salvador – playing with his thin and long moustache, grabbed my attention. Placed below, his quote: *I don't do drugs. I am a drug,* painted an elusive smile on my face.

Suddenly, sharp pain in my nostrils made me forget about my aching tooth. Salvador's moustache had sprouted out of the screen and gone for my brain! In agony, I stood up, distraught, bellowing like a deer in mating season, with my mobile dangling from my nose on those swirling tendrils. The pendulum of madness! When the painter's facial hairs reached my frontal lobe, the time and space melted like the watches in his painting. I fell to the floor. My soul, fed up with my nastily itching brain, left the convulsing body and rushed up like a helium balloon, caught by the ceiling. As if gravity reversed direction, up was down and down was up. But left and right remained the same.

A distant voice in my head shouted: "Get him out! Get him out! Now!" The balloon burst and everything turned black, apart from a small red light in the bottom left corner that enticed me with the scent of Italian fresh-tomato sauce. I swam towards it in a frog-like style and squeezed myself through to the other side.

"Mr President, he's back," said one of many apron-wearing men to a bearded guy sitting behind an impressive desk with American flags behind. I knew this face! It was Philip X. Dickson, a legendary sci-fi author! Tied to a chair, gagged, bristling with plastic tubes that seeped varicoloured potions into and out of me, all I wanted was to clarify the meaning of the last sentence of his most famous novel, *Ubiquity*. But the muzzle didn't let me produce anything better than an unintelligible mumble.

Dickson approached me and said: "Try harder! You're the last hope to stop this BLOODY INVASION!" He hadn't bothered to remove the gag, so I just nodded. "Dr Salvador," he looked towards the Spanish maniac who brought me there, "hit him with another impulse."

The painter, apparently also a doctor, pranced towards me, swinging a curly cable. He stuck it into my left nostril.

"What are the levels of the telepathic-precog aura?" President Dickson asked.

"Sixty point eight ubiks per cubic metre," replied Salvador.

"We have to make sure it works this time! Turn it up!" the President ordered, pointing a remote control at me.

"It might be dangerous."

"I know, but we have to take the risk. Give him one hundred, now!"

A drop of sweat ran down my nose. A laser beam flashed. A blink of an eye followed. An infinitesimal piece of space-time later (or further?) my head was a star with its own planetary system. The rest of my body had ceased to exist. Effectively, I was just a ball of fire. I heard a crunch. The surface of one of the planets cracked in a cloud of dust, pushed from the inside by an enormous hand. A tree-legged, four-armed and two-headed beast got out and shook the soil off its wrinkled body. Drops of sweat froze under its hairy armpits. Each head had its own eye: only one, bloodshot, purple irises, slightly convex, goofy-looking. Each mouth drooled with thick saliva. The creature stretched out one of its arms into space. Its massive fingers grabbed the planet's pink moon. The beast made a series of swings like a cricket player and threw "the ball" toward me.

"No!" I shouted. The moon travelled at an impossible speed. I didn't have time to close my mouth.

I heard a click. A laser beam flashed. A blink of an eye followed. I found myself in a dental chair.

"Your jaw will be numb for at least two more hours. If you feel pain, take paracetamol. This should help. You're free to go unless you have any more questions," said the dentist. I didn't reply, perplexed by the unexpected turn of events I'd just experienced. When my tongue located a gap in the lower row of my teeth on the left, a temporary unification of dream and reality into a higher reality (a surreality?), struck me as a plausible explanation. But I couldn't be sure of anything, including my reasoning.

When I returned home, still dazed and confused, I sprawled on the sofa and lit up an irresponsibly well-deserved cigarette.

I switched on the TV. Neither the reality show nor the football game seemed interesting at all. My belly growled with hunger and anger so I went to the kitchen. As you have probably guessed, the fridge was as empty as my stomach. Apart from five jars of Polish mustard I buy in bulk.

There was a leaflet on the floor. *Pizza Hot Delivery 24h. It must've fallen out of the bin.* I browsed through the menu while dialling their number.

"Halo, it's *Pizza Hot*, how can I help you?" said a woman on the phone.

"Hi, I would like to place an order, as you may have guessed."

"Yes sir, I've guessed that. I've also guessed what you want to order."

"What is it?"

"*Shrooms Extra Large with Spaghetti on Top*, and coke. The mobile network distorts your aura, so I'm not sure if it's Diet Coke, Coke Zero or the regular one."

"Maybe Zero."

"OK."

"I don't need to give you my address, do I?"

Her tone of voice changed dramatically. "Of course not! I'm a well-trained precog!"

"I'm sorry, I didn't mean to—" I was embarrassed.

"You people think that anyone could do this job, right?"

"I'm sorry."

"You should be! You know I could put you on the list!"

"No, please. Don't do that!" The last thing I needed was to be on the fucking list. I was hungry. I needed food. "I'm sorry. I really respect your profession."

"Alright. It's your last warning. Our driver will knock at your door three times."

"What's the password?"

"Murmurations. It'll take thirty to thirty-one minutes."

I returned to the room and stared out the window at the trees bent by the wind saturated with the piss of autumn weather.

Knock, knock.

I glanced through the peephole. There was a man with a pizza. He wore a baseball cap; *Pizza Hot* was written on it; it felt legit but I asked anyway, just in case: "What do you call a large group of birds, usually starlings, flying and changing direction together?"

"Murmurations."

I opened the door. The delivery guy smiled at me. "*Shrooms Extra Large with Spaghetti on Top* for you sir."

"And my coke?"

"She said you wanted zero coke."

"I think she meant Coke Zero.'

"Well, too late."

"Well, forget about your tip then."

"What tip?"

"I don't know."

"Neither do I. So, bye, enjoy your meal."

I put the pizza on the table in the living room. The smell wafting out of the box was mesmerising but one thing was missing: Polish mustard! So I quickly took it from the fridge. Back in the living room, I poured the mustard onto the pizza and spread it over the round surface with my bare hands. And I licked my fingers, purring with pleasure. *Like ambrosia.*

I lit up another cigarette. Halfway through the third puff, I turned on the news channel.

Shivers ran down my spine when a disturbed speaker announced in a trembling voice: "BREAKING NEWS! Vlad Dracula wins the election in Romania. Fresh-blood markets are in turmoil."

Hearing that, I recalled President Dickson's words: *You're the last hope to stop this BLOODY INVASION!*

My mobile phone rang. It was a private number. At that moment I finally grasped the ambiguous ending of *Ubiquity,* Dickson's most famous novel: *This has only just begun.*

GONE WITH THE TWINS

You're leaving it all behind, literally. You're on the train you've just caught at the last minute. The door's just closed behind you. You were running, it's summer, over thirty degrees Celsius, and your breath hasn't stopped sprinting yet, so you're trying to catch it while your hands rest on your bent knees and sweat drips lazily from your chin. But you're smiling.

You sit down while the village where you grew up, where you went to school, where you found your first love and first job (at your family's company), where your parents live (just two streets away), where your auntie lives (just three streets away), with one pub, where every day is the same, where everything is slow and predictable is moving away faster and faster. *Sayonara! Hasta la vista! Do svidaniya!* You want to be gone forever.

Nineteen next month, you've been fed up with your family's surveillance for too long. You couldn't take it any longer. You'll prove them wrong. You're convinced. It's time for changes. That's why you're moving to the big city. Your parents want to control you with their money and they've got plenty of it, so you took some with you. *Money is freedom.*

You get off the train at London Bridge Station. You walk to a hostel, check in, drop your bag, and go out. The human swarm sucks you into a tiny alley by the river. You're a part of it now, following its rhythm. *So exciting!*

Music breaks through the dense cacophony of the crowd. You know this song. It's *Break on Through (To the Other Side)* by The Doors but in Spanish! *Abrirse Camino (Al Otro Lado).*

The deep female voice belongs to a curly black haired young woman wearing loose trousers adorned with yellow fractal shapes and a skimpy black top revealing her flat belly. The diva rocks her hips accompanied by the psychedelic moans of an electric guitar, an old black Stratocaster. *What a classic!* You watch the fingers. They sway you with a wild solo. Up and down the frets and your spine. A sharp slide with an aggressive vibrato breaks a string. This is the end. You think it's awesome to finish a song this way. *The real art!*

Finally, you look at the guitarist's face and, to your surprise, he looks eerily similar to the singer. You compare their elegant noses, stoned eyes and tanned cheeks. *The same!* But hairstyles are different. Both sides of his head are shaven, leaving a strip of red hair in the centre. They must be twins. Beautiful twins. You don't know which one you like more.

"*Gracias, gracias,*" she says to the microphone while people drop coins and notes to a hat lying in front of them. You give them twenty. Two times. They're happy to see that. You tell them how cool they are, your name, where you're from, and all about the big-city adventure. They listen attentively.

"What are your names?" you ask.

"Pablo."

"Laura."

"Are you twins?"

"Yes, but we were born on different dates. Pablo just before midnight and I just after."

"That's awesome." *What are the chances?*

"Thank you," says Laura. "Where do you live?"

"At the moment, I'm staying in a hostel."

"So you're looking for a room, right?" asks Laura and you nod. "Our flat mate is moving out today. You could come tomorrow at midnight to see the place."

"Can you text me the address?"

"No, you have to remember. It's twenty-five Councillor Street in Camberwell. Will you come?" Her emerald eyes are staring at you. His emerald eyes are staring at her.

"Yes, at midnight," you say.

They leave for a party but don't ask if you'd like to come with them.

#

The next day it's Sunday, so you go to Hyde Park, to the Speakers' Corner. You argue with Muslims about Islam and Christians about Christianity and with a guy dressed up as Lenin about communism. Free speech in action. Then sightseeing. Soho, Camden, Brick Lane. *A little boring to be honest.*

Once you're back to the hostel, an Italian tourist asks if you want to buy weed. He's leaving and can't take it with him to the airport so you accept his generous offer.

At the hostel's pub, you have a couple of pints with two Australians. They tell you about their weekend in Amsterdam and the gigantic spiders living in their house in Sydney. You're intrigues and want to know more, so you share a joint with them. It's not a *crime* to find the *rhyme*. Pretending to be *kangaroos*, they deliver terrifying *news*: they don't have Foster's in Australia! "I can't believe it!" you say. "Foster's is the most popular Australian beer in the UK!" You're completely shocked. The *time* goes *fast* and at *last,* you check your phone. 11 pm. According to the internet, Camberwell is not that far away, just a forty-five minute walk.

Yes, *time* is a *crime rhyme*. And time is *money, honey*!

"It was nice to meet you," you say to the marsupials, putting your headphones on. Jazz. As if hovering over the pavements, through busy roads, dark streets and subways, you're zigzagging a little drunk and high under the full moon. (Wait. It's not full – you just imagine it. You've always had a creative imagination – so you're not entirely sure.)

You turn right off Camberwell Road, passing by a permanently closed pet shop and a 24h Food and Wine. A shady guy asks if you want to buy some weed. You say that you've already got some. And he says you look lost and asks where you're going, so you say: "Twenty-five Councillor Street."

"I know where it is. I'll show you."

You walk next to the guy; you smile at him and he smiles back, revealing a missing tooth and licking his lips.

You turn left by a basketball court and then to the right. A fox crosses the street.

"It's here," he says, pointing at the door, "Take my number. I can deliver." After you do, he walks away. It's 11:50 pm. You still have ten minutes, so you walk back to the basketball court and pretend to be Jordan. Finally, you knock on the door of the number twenty-five.

"*Bienvenido!* Welcome!" says Laura.

"Hi, we're glad you could make it," says Pablo.

The flat is ramshackle and smells of weed and tobacco. And you love the walls too; they're painted with fractal shapes. A dreamcatcher hangs in the kitchen above a fridge full of beers proudly presented to you. You take one. *Pss.* Moist lips. You still love Foster's.

"And this could be your room," says Laura, taking you down a narrow corridor; you almost kick Pablo's electric guitar leaning against the wall. *What a classic!* You want to learn how to play. She pushes a creaking door and lets you in. It's all you need: the wardrobe is big enough, the bed is not so creaky (it's important because you want to have a lot of sex) and the dusty desk with an office-style chair – you sit on it and adjust the height – now it's OK too.

"Do you like it?" asks Pablo.

"I do," you say, spinning.

"Now, you'll have to pass the Test," says Laura.

What test? You can't wait to find out.

You return to the kitchen and sit at the table. Laura sits in front of you, Pablo is standing by the sink.

"Thank you for arriving on time," says Pablo.

"Why do you think I asked you to come at midnight?" asks Laura.

"Actually, I was considering many options and I've come to the conclusion that you're a satanic cult and for some reason midnight is the most appropriate time to sacrifice an innocent human being. You know, cut their throat and drink their blood."

"Are you innocent?" asks Laura, giving you a sharp look, *as sharp as a machete.*

"No, I'm not," you reply, cheekily.

"So you have nothing to worry about," says Pablo, taking out a shiny knife from a drawer.

"Why midnight then?" you say, paying attention to Pablo's hands.

"To ask you about it. To see what you can come up with. If you're creative enough to live with us," says Pablo, slicing a tomato.

"Did you like my answer?"

"So so. You could've tried harder," says Laura, offering you a cigarette. You take it and light it up with a puff *as deep as the Mariana Trench.* In your head, you're proud of your unconventional similes but not sure if the twins would like them too. You don't want to embarrass yourself. You don't know their sense of humour so you decide not to share it, at least not now. *Just in case...*

"Why do you like The Doors?" asks Pablo.

"Psychedelic music, crazy lyrics, charismatic leader."

"Interesting order. I like that," says Laura.

"Do you want to be really psychedelic?" asks Pablo.

"Of course," you say. *The big-city adventure!*

"Do you have five hundred for the rent?" asks Laura and you hand her the cash. Pablo throws the knife into the sink and grabs his mobile.

"Hey, it's Pablo. Can you deliver?" he asks someone over the phone.

"What you need?" You can hear the voice of his caller.

"As usual, but double. We're hungry, so hurry up," says Pablo and hangs up.

"Does it mean I'm in?" you ask.

"Yeah," replies Laura.

# #

You've been partying hard with your new flat mates since you moved in four days ago. Four days on mushrooms, pills, weed and alcohol. Now you lie in bed, twisted and thirsty. *Alcohol is the worst*, you think, and you're right. You're a zombie. Insomnia pulls your consciousness on a verge of paranoia when you hear the creaking bed in Laura's room. You hope they're not having sex. *They're twins!* That would be too much. If that's true, you'll move out. You have some values.

Finally, when you dip into a shallow dream, somebody knocks on the front door. It's like a hammer banging on your forehead. You check the time and can't believe it's afternoon. To be sure, you pull the curtains. The sun's rays are like lasers.

Walking down the corridor, you almost throw up. Your body is about to collapse but the hammer keeps banging, so you have no choice but to open the door.

A bald, muscular man pushes himself in. He's drunk and strong.

"Who the fuck are you?" he asks but you say nothing. "Where are they, fucking Manuel and Manuela? Where are they?"

Laura and Pablo get out of their rooms slowly; they're zombies too.

"Where's my money?" asks the man. "This laptop is mine now!"

"No way," says Pablo and takes the laptop off the table. "What money are you talking about?"

"Rent!"

"We've already paid you! It was last week. You forgot?" says Laura. "I gave it to you. Don't you remember? On Thursday. Come on, Mark. You must remember."

Mark is confused: he's scratching his head.

"She paid you last week," says Pablo.

Mark grabs Pablo's hand and swiftly twists his arm,

pushing him to his knees. The laptop hits the floor.

"Don't chat shit! Rent! Or I'll break your fucking arm!"

Skinny Pablo looks so hopeless, like a boy being punished by a pathological father.

"Let him go," says Laura and looks at you with her emerald eyes.

"How much is it?" you ask and instantly regret it.

"Two thousand! You have money?" Mark releases Pablo's arm and walks towards you like a raging bull. He pushes you to the wall and says, spitting into your face: "Where's the money? In your room?" You nod. He pulls your ear. "Take me there!"

Back in your room, you're not sure if you want to pay for them. "I don't have any money. I lied."

"Bullshit!" He checks under the bed and in the wardrobe. "Where is it?" he shouts at you.

"I don't have any money!" you repeat in vain when he spots a gap between the wardrobe and the wall. You should've hidden it better.

"It's here!" he says, smiling, and easily pushes the almost empty wardrobe aside to find a suitcase. He takes it out and opens it. "Oh fuck, it's my lucky day!"

"That's not your money!" shouts Laura, standing by the door.

"Fuck off!" replies Mark and walks out the room, suitcase in hand. He pushes her. She falls to the floor. You follow him, mad, wanting to kill the bastard! You grab the electric guitar, make a swing and smash it on his head. Now he, too, is lying on the floor, not moving, blocking the corridor.

Pablo checks Mark's pulse and says: "He's not breathing. He's dead."

This is rock and roll! No, it's more than that. You've just killed a man. *This is Norwegian black metal!*

Pablo and Laura are shouting in Spanish and all you understand is *policía, prisión* and *asesinato*. But that's enough to know what they mean. You're in trouble! Your hangover becomes unbearable. Your mind is foggy. You wish this was just a computer game, *press X in the top right corner...*

Pablo takes the suitcase, puts it on the table and asks: "How much is inside?"

"Fifty thousand," you say.

Pablo opens the suitcase and Laura takes a bundle of notes out of it. She smells the cash with bliss on her face. When they start to talk in Spanish again, you look at the body awkwardly lying on its belly, at its bald head with a red patch. You hit him very hard but the guitar is fine. You notice a metallic object sticking out of his trousers pocket. Pablo and Laura are busy with themselves, so you use this opportunity and approach the body. It's a gun, a small silver pistol with a brown wooden grip. A dark thought of killing them both strikes you. It's tempting. Nobody knows you've been living here apart from them and they don't even have your mobile number. You have to be quick. You have to take the pillow from the sofa and press it to Pablo's belly, and shoot. He's stronger, so he has to go first. And then Laura. And then you'll pack your stuff and go back to the hostel. Nobody will ever know.

"What did you find there?" asks Laura, bending over you.

"A gun. Look." You panic and give it to her. She puts it on the table.

"Where's this money from?" asks Pablo.

"I took it from my parents."

They stare at you with their arms crossed, lifting their left eyebrows, so similar, like clones, and you wonder if they think about kidnapping you for ransom.

"How rich are your parents?" asks Laura.

"Doesn't matter. We have to get rid of the body. You can take this fifty thousand if you help me," you say. Money is not a problem for you, it's never been. The body is!

"We will," says Laura. You're not sure what she meant.

"So what's your plan?" asks Pablo.

"I don't know," you say. Leaning against the wall, you

slowly slide down to the floor and grab your head.

"I have an idea," says Laura. She opens a cupboard and takes out a couple of screwdrivers, a hammer and a small saw. Now, all this equipment is lying on the table next to the suitcase but the gun is not there any more.

"Or we can dissolve him in the bathtub," says Pablo. You've seen it in a film. A glance at the body makes you throw up.

"Fucking hell! You have to clean it. It stinks," says Pablo. You wash your face in the kitchen sink but leave the vomit on the floor.

"Car!" Laura says.

She checks Mark's pockets and finds the car keys. Then, she looks out the window. You join her. There's a van parked in front of your house. She smiles. It must be his.

"We have to fake a car accident," she says with *a light bulb above her head, like in a cartoon.*

"You're right. He was drunk. The police may believe it," you say.

"I know a good place," adds Pablo.

A team spirit's hanging in the air. You notice that the middle finger of Pablo's left hand is dislocated.

"How do we transport the body to the car?" asks Laura, and all of you look at the table where the tools are lying as if waiting for you to use them.

"I have a better idea, we can use my wardrobe. I haven't even put any clothes in yet," you say.

"It won't be easy," says Pablo, and he's right. He pulls his dislocated finger, screaming and sweating, but it won't move.

"Let me help you," says Laura. "Are you ready? Three, two—"

"Aaaaaa!" shouts Pablo.

#

It's almost midnight when you're somewhere between

Eastbourne and Brighton close to the cliffs, driving the van with Laura sitting next to you and Pablo behind. Mark's body is at the back, in the wardrobe-coffin.

Pablo has the gun and you wonder if he'd use it against you.

"What are you going to do with fifty thousand pounds?" you ask. "Going back to Spain?"

"We'll buy a farm in Guatemala and grow weed," replies Laura.

You stop the van on a forest path where no one can see you behind the dense wall of trees.

"We'll wait for you here," says Laura.

"Will you?" you ask, but there's no answer.

"Let's move the landlord," says Pablo, opening the side sliding door of the van. You jump in and open the wardrobe. Then the three of you pull out the body. Laura helps you to place him on the driver's seat. She slaps Mark's indifferent face and says: "Listen to me! If the police asked, you say: 'I was drunk and lonely, so I killed myself.' OK?" Then she looks at you. "You're free to go." Pablo pats you on your shoulder for encouragement.

You adjust the seat to make some space for yourself and sit behind the wheel, in between Mark's legs. His head collapses on you and his protruding tongue wets your neck. You look into his dead eyes and put the key into the ignition while Laura and Pablo are waving at you and sending kisses.

You drive away towards the main road with your hands trembling like a guitar string and your mouth dry *like the Sahara, or even the Atacama!*

This is it! You turn sharply to the left. Through a meadow, you're heading towards the cliff. The van is shaking when you gain speed. Mark's head bounces off yours. You'll have a bump near your temple. You're getting close to the precipice, so you open the door, put the gearbox in neutral, push Mark to your left, and jump out of the speeding vehicle. You roll on the ground and feel like you want to vomit. Your right elbow and left knee are aching but no bones are broken. You're lucky!

The van is slowing down! It stops halfway through its length, hanging over the cliff. "No!" you shout, hitting the ground with your fist. You have no choice but to finish it.

You push hard, gasping and swearing. Yes, you can do it. "Come on, fucking gravity! Help me! Do your part!" The back of the van goes up slowly and you step back. You exhale with relief. This is your moment. You step further back to gain momentum and run towards the van. It's easier than you thought. The van falls and hits the rocks five hundred feet below, exploding. You admire the flames proud of the accomplished mission. Like Lara Croft or James Bond. But what are you going to do now? You can't just return home. You want to go to Guatemala with the twins. *Maybe they're waiting for me?* You have to check.

#

The path is dark and you see almost nothing, so you shout: "Hey! Are you there?"

"Yes, we're here by the fallen tree. Come!" You follow Laura's voice. They're waiting for you, sitting on a trunk with the suitcase in front of them. Pablo stands up and says, "Listen, we have to talk about the money."

"Let's talk about money, *no problemo, muchachos*," you say.

He takes out the gun and points at your forehead. Paralysed by fear, you close your eyes.

"*Sayonara! Hasta la vista!*" says Pablo.

"*Do svidaniya,*" you reply.

Click. You heard the trigger but nothing happened. *Am I dead?* They both laugh, so you open your eyes and see a flame coming out of a gun's barrel. It's just a lighter.

"Do you want to smoke a joint?" asks Laura.

#

Two years later, the Pacific Ocean cools down your feet.

You go deeper, up to your waist. The waves are gentle.

"Your mum's just called!" Pablo, standing on the beach and waving a mobile phone, yells at you.

"Fuck," you say to yourself. You know you have to speak to her about money. You spent the first fifty thousand in six months, so you had no choice but to ask your mother for help. She's been sending you money without your dad knowing for over a year and now she wants to visit you.

Laura thinks that, at some point, she'll have to come. "We can't postpone it forever," she keeps saying. You trust Laura's judgement. She taught you how to speak to your mother and make her send money. Laura is very good at manipulating people. She says you have to be charming and a little mysterious. Give compliments but scarcely, so they're worth more. And you should be cheeky at times, making sure they feel guilty. "So you could give them one more chance if they admit it's their fault," she once said. *She's so smart!*

You practised role-playing with both of them to master these skills. You played your mother. That was fun. You studied her online profile with Laura and she created strategies for you.

Now, when you call your mother from your paradisiacal wooden beach cottage, you know what to do: you let her talk. She tells you she misses you. She's sorry for all the things that happened in the past. She knows you need your freedom. She knows she tried to control you. She won't do that any more. Awkward silence. She just wants to spend time with you.

"I just want to spend time with you," your mum says.

"You want to spend time with me? Don't forget: TIME IS MONEY, HONEY!" you say, proud of your sarcasm. That's how shameless you've become.

IGUANA

Veronica entered the bedroom completely naked. Her super-hot husband was lying in bed. A laptop on his belly, busy with work, he didn't seem to notice her at all.

She lay down next to him and caressed his neck, whispering: "Patrick, I love you. I want you."

"I love you too, but I'm exhausted."

It didn't stop her advances. She smoothed her hand down his chest and abdomen. But when she tried to get into his pants, he stopped her and said: "I promise, as soon as I complete this report, I'll be all yours. Please, don't be mad." He kissed her forehead.

"I'm not mad. I'm just a little—"

"Do you want to watch a documentary or something?" He saved the changes in the spreadsheet and opened the browser.

"OK, let's watch a documentary," she replied, disappointed, looking out the window at a tree tousled by gusts of wind soaked with the tears of English autumn weather.

Patrick had lost interest in sex in recent months, blaming the amount of work he had at his new position of fundraising officer at an environmental charity. He just had to make a good impression. It was overwhelming but worth the effort, and it wouldn't last long, he would say with a reassuring smile. The importance of first impressions...

"Nature and wildlife?" he asked.

"Up to you. I trust your judgement."

Straddling the equator, six hundred miles off the western coast of South America, lies a unique world: Galapagos Islands. It was here where Charles Darwin encountered a community of creatures unlike any other in the world.

Squeezing his hand under the duvet, she recalled the day they met in a salsa class. A horrible dancer, but his eyes..., she'd thought. Now, he was next to her, but somehow distant.

When mating, the male iguana clasps the back of the female's neck in his jaws, holding her down, before inseminating her with one of his two penises. Five weeks later, the female is ready to lay, usually five to eight eggs.

Married last year, they had decided not to have children as there were already enough people in the world, more than enough. Eight billion! At least seven billion too many. No planet in the Solar System could sustain those numbers, certainly not Earth.

Ecosystems in Galapagos are strongly influenced by climate, that's why climate change could affect biodiversity across the Islands. Changes in temperatures and rainfall interfere with the iguanas' ability to regulate their temperature and consequently reduce nesting success.

"Perhaps we could visit Galapagos. Would you like to go?" she asked.

"We could do that. Why not?" he replied indifferently.

"So when are we going?" She paused the video, forcing him to pay attention.

"Are you serious?"

"Deadly serious."

"Well, I have this report to—"

"I know, I know. I meant when you finish it. You will finish it one day, right?"

"Of course, I will."

"So when it's done, we'll go. We could use some quality time in a tropical country to relax, enjoy."

"You're right, we could, but let's sleep now. I'm absolutely knackered." He closed the laptop and reached for the bedside lamp to turn it off.

"No. I want to see what happens to this lizard, and you have to watch it with me." She pressed play. The camera took a close-up of the iguana's face while a stream of salt gushed out of its nose.

They developed salt glands that remove the salt from their blood and deposit it in the nostrils.

#

The arid surface of the tiny Baltra Island emerged from the blues of the Pacific Ocean.

After the passport control at the airport, Veronica and Patrick, together with a group of other tourists, boarded a ferry that transported them to Santa Cruz Island. On the other side of the strait, a man holding a sheet with their names was waiting by a car.

"Veronica and Patrick! *¡Bienvenidos a Galapagos!* I'll take you to your hotel. How was your journey?"

As the car rode uphill, the vegetation changed rapidly in front of their eyes. The dry bushes gave way to a lush tropical forest.

"How is that possible?" asked Veronica.

"We reached a higher altitude. The microclimate here is different. Galapagos is a place that will keep surprising you," explained the driver.

They stopped in front of a cosy hotel in a romantic village by the seaside.

#

Veronica lay down in bed and took off her t-shirt. "Can you help me with my bra, darling?"

"Shall we go to the beach?" he asked as if he thought she wanted to change into her bikini.

"Yeah. Let's go to the beach."

#

Lazy waves hummed, bouncing off the shore sparsely sprinkled with dark volcanic rocks while Veronica stepped down wooden stairs built over the dunes, blinded by the white sand of Tortuga Bay Beach that reflected the equatorial heat.

Patrick ran straight into the ocean, laughing like a child.

Veronica followed him, but she stopped when the cold water cooled down her feet and sat down, allowing the waves to pet her buttocks.

A motionless reptile leered at her from between the rocks. She almost missed it as its eerie blackness blended in with the surrounding. *Like a lifeless dead indeed,* she thought, while approaching the scaly creature. She waved her hand in front of its eyes, but there was no reaction, just dumb indifference. Or perhaps, belligerent, cold-blooded cheekiness? Or simply sadness? She wasn't sure. "Are you Godzilla's cousin?"

A wet, chilly touch on her back followed by "BOOO!" shouted into her ear, snapped her out of the lizard's gaze. It was Patrick, having childish fun. She lost her balance and landed on the rock just in front of the iguana, scratching her palms. Patrick almost died of laughter.

"Very funny," she said. "Help me."

When he grabbed her bleeding hand, she pulled him down. He fell on the lizard's tail. The annoyed animal sneezed and a ray of a white jelly liquid erupted off its snout, blinding him.

"What the fuck are you doing? Do you want to kill me?" he shouted, rubbing his eyes. Red drops were dripping from his nose.

"You got what you deserved! You were laughing at me!"

#

"I don't like this fish," said Patrick.
"Mine is fine."

#

When Patrick woke up the next day, his digestive and excretory systems were in a melancholic mood, so Veronica went out on her own. She headed towards *Las Grietas,* a place advertised in the tourist guide as "Santa Cruz's Best

Swimming Hole!" The dramatic setting of emerald green water trapped in between high volcanic walls comforted her.

She took out the tourist guide. *The water at* Las Grietas *is around ten metres deep, and seven metres wide. There is no lifeguard on duty, so only enter the water if you are a good swimmer, or with a floating device.*

Only in a bikini, she stood on the edge. It could've been ten to fifteen metres down to the water level. She took a big step back to gain momentum and counted down.

"Three, two, one! Hey ho! Let's go!" She made two quick steps towards the precipice, but in the last second, she hesitated. Was it fear or the desperate voice of reason? It didn't matter. It was too late. Her feet slipped, and the gravity pulled her down into the unknown.

The sudden collision with the cold water was like a shot of adrenaline. An electrifying sensation swirled its way through her body.

#

"How is your belly? Are you feeling better?" she asked.
"A little. I packed our bags for tomorrow."
"Oh, great."

#

On a speedboat, somewhere between Santa Cruz and Isabela islands, their faces, burned by laser-like sun rays, enjoyed the gentle touch of the wind.
"Sorry for yesterday," he said.
"Accepted. But what about the day before?"
"Also my fault."
"OK. So let's forget about it."
"Thank you."
She took the tourist guide and read out loud: " 'Sierra Negra is a large shield volcano at the southeastern end of

Isabela Island that rises to an altitude of 1124 metres.' Are you ready for the hike?"

"Sure." He flipped his tongue.

#

When they arrived in Isabela, in the late afternoon, a beach bar by the harbour played salsa.

"Do you remember when we first met?" asked Patrick.

"How could I forget? You step on my toes a hundred times."

"We should drop our stuff in the hotel and come here for a drink."

"Good idea."

When they returned to the bar, they sat in a corner.

"*Bienvenidos!* What would you like to drink? We have delicious cocktails," said a waiter.

"Can you recommend your favourites?" asked Veronica.

"Sure. I like Iguana, a delicious mixture of coconut rum, vodka, Blue Curacao, and pineapple juice. Would you like to try?"

"I would," said Patrick.

"I also like Sex on the Beach," added the waiter, winking at Veronica. "It's made of—"

"I know what's made of. One for me, please," she replied.

After a couple of drinks, Patrick asked her to dance. He grabbed her hands decisively, and they engaged their bodies into undulating moves.

"Where did you learn this?" He ignored the question, looking into her eyes. Maybe she's had too much alcohol and her imagination played pranks on her, but there was something wild, animalistic in his gaze.

"We could go for a walk and see what happens," he whispered enigmatically.

Under the full moon, a little drunk, holding their hands, smoothing the wet sand with their bare feet, they zigzagged their way to a cosy spot by a palm tree where they lay in an embrace. He ripped off her clothes. He bit her neck. He scratched her back. She loved it.

Lava blasted out of the volcano in a cloud of dust and rocks. Running down the mountainside, it sowed death and destruction.

#

Still drunk from last night's events, Veronica stretched lazily in bed with a blissful smile. The beauty of the morning sunshine called her, so she stood up and went out onto the see-view balcony.

"Patrick, wake up! Come here. It's so beautiful. Patrick!" He was still in bed, lying on his side and facing the wall. "Patrick?" She returned to the bed and pulled his shoulder towards her. His indifferent, motionless face was emaciated, with dark patches of festering, slimy scales. She shook his body in a desperate attempt to bring him back to life. "Patrick! Wake up!"

An excruciating spasm assaulted her belly from the inside. She curled up, howling in pain. "Help! Help!"

The pain reduced its intensity. She stood up clumsily, put on a bathrobe and stormed out of the room.

Downstairs, a group of people glued to the TV watched the volcano vomiting red, liquid rocks. *Desastre natural en Galápagos después de la erupción volcánica.*

"Call an ambulance!"

"What happened?" asked the receptionist.

"My husband's lying in bed with a lizard face! He's not moving."

"What room is it?"

"Number ten."

Two men, the hotel staff, ran to her room and she followed them.

"Nobody is here," said one of the men.

"He was here. Just a minute ago. Patrick?" she said.

"*Está loca,*" added the other one.

"No, no, no. I'm not crazy." she replied. "I swear he was here. Patrick! Patrick!" Leaning against the wall, she slowly slid down to the floor, grabbed her head in disbelief, and threw up.

#

"*Señora...* Sorry, can you repeat your surname?" asked the police officer who arrived at the hotel, looking at her in a bizarre, unhuman way that reminded her of the way Patrick had done the night before.

"Veronica Banks."

"*Señora* Banks, are you saying that when you woke up, your husband was dead?" He was snooping around the room.

"He wasn't moving. He wasn't breathing."

"And then he disappeared?"

"Yes. I know it sounds weird, but it's true." She decided not to mention the lizard face.

"Hmm, zombie?"

"Are you kidding? My husband is missing and you're making stupid jokes?"

"My apologies. When did you see him alive for the last time?"

"Last night, when we returned to the room."

"What time was it?" His intrusive eyes leered at her from under bushy eyebrows.

"Around midnight. I'm not sure exactly. Maybe it was later than that."

"Were you drinking alcohol?"

"What are you suggesting?"

"I'm just asking. So were you or not?" Veronica nodded. "I thought so."

"I'm really worried."

"I'd really like to help you, *Señora* Banks, but it's too early to launch a missing person investigation. We need at least forty-eight hours unless something indicates a person could be a victim of a crime, and I can't see any of that. Also, we don't have many resources at the moment. Fire is raging through the forest. Ten people died last night as a result of the eruption, and many are injured. Rocks fell on their houses. It was horrible. So, there's not much I can do right now. I'm sorry."

"But—"

"Perhaps *Señor* Banks was upset and just wanted to be alone. It happens sometimes."

"But he left his phone and passport in the room. Even the wallet."

"Has everything been OK between you two lately?"

"How dare you ask?"

"It's just my job. So OK or not OK?"

"Everything was fine."

"I'm sure he'll be back soon. But just in case, I'll come in the evening to speak to you. Hopefully to both of you."

#

The volcanic eruption didn't directly affect the small village where Veronica was staying.

After the officer left, she went out to look for Patrick on her own. It was morning, so the restaurants and bars were still closed. No traffic. Only a few tourists strolled the street. One after another, she showed them a photo of her husband.

"Nein."

"Nie."

"Net."

"Non."

She headed to the beach. The sun was already strong.

When people fall in love, they often feel butterflies in their stomachs. Veronica felt the opposite: as if she carried stones in her lower abdomen. She felt nauseous.

"Patrick! Patrick!" she kept shouting as she was walking along the beach.

She stopped at the place where they had made love. "Patrick!"

An iguana came out of the bush. It was at least twice bigger than any other iguana she'd seen so far. And way more muscular. It headed towards her.

"What do you want? Leave me alone!"

But it didn't. It just moved faster.

She felt dizzy. The world was spinning. She fell to the ground.

The scaly body brushed her legs. With the last of her strength, she stood up. The lizard stared at her with its indifferent, reptilian eyes.

She ran.

#

The sun was melting into the ocean outside the hotel room window.

"Knock, knock. *Señora* Banks, may I come in?" asked the officer.

"Yes." She was in pain again. Her belly was swollen.

"You don't look well. Stomach problems?"

"Do you know anything about my husband?" She lay in bed.

"I'm afraid I do not."

"So what were you doing?"

"The volcano killed another twenty people. Trust me, we are very busy."

"I'm sorry to hear that."

"Have you had a chance to think about you and your husband?"

"What do you mean?"

"Back home, has he recently started coming home late? Perhaps a new hobby? And you were not invited to join?"

"No."

"Are you sure?"

"Well, he has a new job and sometimes he stays late. You're right. I mean, you're not completely wrong."

"Demanding boss?"

"Yes."

"Is she a woman?"

"Yes."

"Hmm. Can I see his phone?"

"Of course." She pointed at a bag in the corner. "In the big pocket."

With the phone in his hand, he sat next to her. "Is there a password?"

"I don't know. Maybe there is."

"What's her name?"

"Whose?"

He looked into Veronica's eyes. "Your husband's boss."

"Rachel."

The officer passed the phone to her. "Type: 'Rachel'."

She typed it. "No. It's not working. It's not 'Rachel'."

"What about 'Password123'?"

"Correct. How did you know?"

"Lucky guess." He moved closer to her to see the screen better. "Go to his email."

Veronica browsed through the apps. "I didn't know my husband uses Hotmail."

"He's hiding something. Click on it."

A strong contraction struck her lower abdomen, putting pressure on her pelvis. Sweat moistened her face. She felt dizzy.

"Come on! What are you waiting for? Do you want me to check?" The officer took her hand, straightened her index finger, and pressed the touchscreen. "There you go! Now go to the search and type 'Rachel'. Or are you too afraid?"

"No, I'm not."

"So do it!"

When she typed the name of her husband's boss, multiple emails appeared on the screen.

"Click on the one with a photo attached," he said. When she did, he burst into laughter. "Nice. I knew he was hiding something, but I didn't expect that! You must be furious. It's so humiliating. Do you need a hug?"

"Fuck!" Another contraction, much stronger, took her breath away when her waters broke. "Aaa!"

"I see you're busy." He stood up. "Do you mind if I watch?"

"Aaa!" The pain was intensive: strong cramping in the abdomen and groin.

"I take it as 'yes'. I'm not a specialist but I think you should push harder."

"Aaa!"

"Keep going! You're doing well."

"Aaa!" In agony, she pushed as hard as she could.

"Well done! You're a mother. Congratulations! You've just laid an egg." He took it from between her legs and put it on her chest. It was the size of a fist. "Ufff, what an aroma. You must be proud!"

"Leave me alone! Help! Somebody help me!"

"Nobody can hear you. Do you know what you should do now? You have to go to the beach, dig a hole, and bury it. Obey the law of nature, woman. This is what good mothers do. Aren't you a good mother?"

"I'm not!" She stood up and lumbered to the balcony. "*Hasta la vista,* baby." There was no mercy. The egg crashed against a palm tree.

#

"Where am I?" asked Veronica.

"You're in the hospital," replied Patrick. His blurry face gradually regained its focus. No signs of scaly patches.

"Hospital?" She lifted her sore body as if she didn't believe him. "So you didn't die?" Strangely, she was a little disappointed. She wanted to ask about the egg but stopped herself at the last moment, slowly releasing that it had never existed. It was all a bad dream. A creation of her fears and insecurities. A puke of the unconscious. Wasn't it?

"Of course I'm not dead. It was just food poisoning. You're the one who almost died. Do you remember?"

"No."

"You went to *Las Grietas* and jumped into the precipice. You almost drowned. If other people hadn't reacted so quickly... I don't even want to think about it."

"Give me your phone." She stretched her hand towards him.

"What? Why do you need my phone? Are you feeling alright? I'd better call the doctor. *Por favor, doctor aquí.*"

"Give me your phone. I need to call somebody."

He unlocked the screen and passed his phone to her. She went to his contact list, picked one, and put it on the loudspeaker. *Beep, beep, beep.*

"Hey sexy!" a female voice answered the call. "Are you already missing me? Cause I am! A lot! Patrick? Are you there?"

Lava blasted out of the volcano in a cloud of dust and rocks. Running down the mountainside, it sowed death and destruction.

BAD RIDDANCE

Lightning bolts illuminate the clouds swirling in the dark sky above the forest.

Alice and Jenny step out of the vehicle and their faces grimace in doubt. Raincoats and wellingtons don't prevent the fury of the storm from shaking them to the bone. Despite their hesitation, they switch on their torches and march into the darkness of the forest path.

After an hour of walking uphill, the madness of the rain doesn't want to surrender and their feet, bogged down in the mud, need a rest. They sit down on a fallen log under a tall oak.

"To be honest, I'm not sure if we're going to find it. I'm knackered. I give up," says Jenny. *Coming here was a fucking stupid idea!* she thinks.

"No, it's there! Look!" says Alice, pointing at a shy glow between the trees. "Let's go!" She stands up.

Jenny takes her time. A deep breath. She puts her hand in her jacket pocket to touch the rosary she's taken "just in case", and whispers a little prayer: "Holy Mother…"

"Hey, are you coming or what?" says Alice, spreading her arms. "Hurry up!" She thinks: *This lazy bitch is so useless!*

"OK, OK. Calm down, boss," replies Jenny. Alice isn't really her boss but it feels as if she was. "Holy Mother…"

They follow this timid glare through the swampy terrain, densely covered with spiky trees and bushes. A branch cuts Alice's cheek, but she isn't bothered, hypnotised by the inconspicuous wooden cottage hidden among the trunks; smoke comes from its chimney.

Wet and shaky, they approach the entrance with reluctance. A distorted-face statue of a winged creature, attached above the doors, leers down at them insolently. Alice knocks on the door.

"Password!" says a hoarse, foreign voice, the "r" sound ominously overemphasised.

"One second," says Alice, browsing through her phone. *"The dire desire, born of fire, brings us here without fear. We are willing to ask for killing. Help us in a sacrifice for a high price. Now, open the door to allow the gore."*

"You asked for it." When the door opens, a tall, muscular man, wearing a black leather coat on a bare torso, invites them in, stepping aside. *"Zdravstvuyte,"* he says and winks. His long facial hair camouflages almost perfectly his yellow teeth when he smiles at them, bolting back the creaky door.

In the corner of the dingy interior, lit with candles, a ferocious-looking old woman in a black hood sits behind a wooden desk and drinks a red liquid. Behind her, shelves bent under the weight of various kinds of jars filled with vividly coloured substances, and kitchen appliances. She stretches her arm towards them.

"Show your respect to Baba Yaga!" says the man.

Jenny almost shits her pants. Alice is excited.

They sit down on stools opposite the woman and kiss her snow-white, wrinkled hand. Baba Yaga's nose, which they now can see in all its glory, is long and pointy, with a dark wart at its end. Her bloodshot eyes penetrate them.

"Why are you here?" asks Baba Yaga. Her breath smells like sulphur.

#

Alexander, the patriarch of the Owen family, lay in bed in an opulent room of his mansion. He was connected to a life support medical equipment that beeped each time his weak heart beat. In recent weeks, his condition had deteriorated rapidly.

Four people stood by his bed: his adult children, Alice and Ben; his second, much younger wife Elizabeth; and his faithful lawyer, Ricardo. Each of them, blinded with the dream of power, thought of nothing but the fortune they believed they deserved to inherit.

When Alexander lifted his soring body, a dark silhouette holding a scythe walked over the threshold. Nobody but him could see it.

"I don't have much time," he said, with a trembling voice, "so listen carefully. Dear Elizabeth, you've been a great relief for my loneliness. I'll always love you."

"I love you too!" said Elizabeth. Her tears smeared her make-up and ran down her face, dripping on the white bedsheet.

"This house will be yours when I'm gone. You'll also be paid a monthly allowance. Enough for the comfortable life you deserve to have."

She kissed his forehead, and stroked his thinning hair. She was moderately content with her husband's decision.

The Grim Reaper, who had already approached the bed, slipped his scythe under the duvet and stabbed Alexander in the foot. The old man howled in pain.

"Alex? What's going on?" asked Elizabeth, trying to play the good wife until the end.

"Darling, it's OK." He took a deep breath. "When it comes to our family business," he spoke with an effort, "I've decided Ben will take over after I'm gone."

"Thank you, dad," said Ben, barely able to hide his satisfaction. His pupils, widened by cocaine, expanded even further making his irises almost disappear, and his left leg started to dance a little.

"What? I'm more qualified than he is! Is it because I'm a woman?" asked furious Alice.

"You're better qualified? You're a delusional drug addict with no shame! Did you think I'd let you destroy my company?" said Alexander. The beeping of the medical equipment increased its frequency.

"I've been back from rehab for six months now! I've been clean since then! And he's a fucking gambler! He'll be the one who ruins it!" said Alice.

"Shut up!" said Ben. His fist clenched.

"You shut up!" she replied. "He's high, look at his eyes!

Right here, right now, he's high. It's not fair. Dad, I deserve to be treated equally!"

Ben wanted to slap her stupid, spoiled face. Punch her. Punch her hard. So she would get what she deserved. But he knew he couldn't in front of his dying father.

"Your behaviour just confirms I'm right. You can keep the beach house and the car. That's it. Ben, the rest is all yours. Ricardo, pass me the paper please," said Alexander to the lawyer.

The ink on the document hadn't yet dried when the Grim Reaper crawled on the bed. "Beelzebub is waiting for you. Sleep my...," he whispered to his victim's ear. The cold pain of the cutting blade was the last thing Alexander felt as a living man.

Alice stormed out of the room, crying over the fortune she believed was meant to be hers. A family portrait hanging in the corridor was the first casualty of the orgy of destruction she was planning. When she finished tearing it into pieces, she went for an ancient-style statue depicting her father as a Roman emperor. It shattered into pieces after crashing onto the marble floor. *Fuck you! Fuck you all!* She recalled rehab, the toughest challenge anyone could face. And now her father had just called her a delusional junkie!

She ran out to the front of the building, the remains of the statue's head in her hand.

"I'll show you what I can do," she murmured through gritted teeth and walked towards Ben's red Ferrari.

The head smashed the windshield and set off the alarm. Alice picked up what appeared to be her late father's nose and began carving vulgar words all over the vehicle.

After she finished drawing a dick on the Ferrari's bonnet, she sat in her yellow Lamborghini parked on the side and lit up a cigarette. She needed soothing and there was only one way she knew.

"What a surprise! My favourite client, Alice Owen. I haven't heard from you for a while," said Dean, her dealer.

"Dean, listen, I'm very hungry! Where can I meet you?"

"Do you want to come to my place?"

"I'm coming now."

"I'm not home now. In an hour?"

Alice glanced at her golden Rolex. "OK. See you there. Don't be late!"

#

"Igor," says Baba Yaga, "can you sort it out?" She's pointing at a hairy spider hanging from the ceiling between terrified Jenny and disgusted Alice. The bearded man catches the string of the cobweb and swings the creature into his mouth. "*Khrustyashchiy*," he says, chewing loudly.

"He said it's crunchy," explains Baba Yaga. "What b—" Her lips twitch: annoyed at being interrupted by Igor's monstrous burp that has just shaken the walls. "Behave yourself! We have guests! Sorry for him."

"That's OK," says Alice. "I've heard worse."

Jenny says nothing. *Holy Mother...*

"Fascinating story. So unfair," says Igor.

"I know," replies Alice. "Terrible. That's why I need your help."

"Do you mind me asking, what business your family runs?" asks the witch.

"We own a chain of *luxury* hotels," replies Alice. She loves pointing out how rich she is.

"More luxurious than this place?" The old woman spreads her arms, presenting the room with pride.

"A little, but not as cosy," says Alice with a wink.

The answer makes the witch laugh.

Jenny is even more terrified now. Not only of the hosts, but also of Alice's confidence when talking to them.

"I'm glad you feel comfortable here," says Baba Yaga. "I honestly thought that only Igor and I liked it. Who told you how to find me?"

Awkward silence. Alice nudges Jenny.

"It was Svetlana," replies Jenny.

"Svetlana? Igor! Svetlana, *dva*," says Baba Yaga. Igor takes a notebook with a pen out of his jacket pocket. He writes something, murmuring: "Svetlana, *dva*."

"Oh, so you also have a reason to get rid of Ben. Am I right, darling?" The old woman stares at Jenny.

#

On a cold and windy evening, heavy drops hit the window of a lavish hotel room where two hot bodies had just been giving each other pleasure, like rabbits, like dogs, like snakes.

"Wow, that was nice," said Ben and got off the bed lithely, still naked. He lit up a thick Cuban cigar and sat on a gold framed armchair, spreading his legs in an obscene exposure. "Now, it's time for you to go."

"Sorry?" asked Jenny, red cheeks, her heart still beating fast, surprised by his words. Normally they would've stayed in a romantic embrace for a little longer.

"I'm bored with you, Jenny," he said matter-of-factly.

"What did you say?" She opened her arms in disbelief.

"We've had fun, but it's over."

It came out of nowhere. She thought things were going well. She'd already told her besties about how sexy and rich he was. *He must be joking!*

"Just please, don't say you really fell in love with me." He blew a smoke ring. "You are, or rather were, in the top three if that makes you feel better. It should. You had tough competition." He stood up to take his smartphone off the table. "Look at this one." He flashed a photo of a woman in a skimpy bikini. "Nice boobs, eh?" He licked his lips. "And she's really good at doing… you know what I mean… This thing, you're not as good as you should be." He pushed the cigar deeper into his mouth to demonstrate what he meant. And then he smiled and stared into Jenny's eyes with satisfaction.

He's really enjoying himself! What a psycho!

"Jenny, you're nothing."

His words hurt. It felt almost physical, as if he kicked her in the stomach.

He blew another smoke ring. "I have no choice but to let you go. Just don't cry, alright? Crying, it's pathetic. You're already crying, fuck. Seriously?"

"I hate you!" She approached him and slapped his derisive face as strongly as she could. He didn't even move, just smiled and stared at her. The satisfaction she'd seen in his eyes turned into something more sinister.

He blew smoke into her face saying: "Get out."

She put on her clothes in a hurry and left the room, slamming the door behind her. *You're going to regret this, you spoiled, entitled piece of shit,* she thought, kicking and banging the wall in the corridor.

"Hey! You may need this," said Ben; he stood in the slightly open door, holding his semi-erect penis in one hand and the umbrella in the other. "It's raining cats and dogs."

Jenny glanced at him with disgust. "Stick it up your arsehole!"

The weather was nasty indeed when she walked out the main door of the hotel. She took a bus. Her anger was gradually turning into sadness and pity. *Stupid girl*, she thought, recalling the dream of the wealthy life Ben would have provided: parties with celebrities, fast cars, champagne baths... The bubble burst with a bang like a champagne cork. It was all gone. *The rich don't respect common people. We're just tools for them, and when they're bored or satisfied, they just get rid of us.*

She wondered how to take revenge. She could go to the media and tell them... What would she tell them? *He raped me!* No, she couldn't lie about that.

Someone had left a local newspaper on the seat next to hers. She picked it up. *Politics. Boring. Sport. Boring...* She flipped through the pages and found the horoscope section. Her zodiac sign was Cancer. *Passion is on your mind today. You could learn some rather surprising things about your loved ones.*

Mercury, the planet of communication, retrogrades in a family-relationship zone, bringing potential major shake-ups to your private life, with the possibility of losing your foundation and emotional security. She couldn't believe how accurate it was. The name of the author, Svetlana, together with her contact details were below the text. Jenny dialled the number.

#

It can't be here, thought Jenny and double checked the address. *Nail salon?*

She entered. It was busy.

"Just a moment, madam," said a lady who Jenny assumed was the manager. The lady said something in Chinese to one of her subordinates. "You'll have to wait five minutes. My colleague is finishing with a client."

"I'm here to meet Svetlana."

"Ah, OK. Svetlana. Follow me."

They entered a dim corridor at the back.

"Svetlana is very good at her job," said the lady. They turn to the left. "Predicts the future, speaks to the dead and demons. Very good. Very, very good." They turned to the right. "When you speak to her, pay attention to her nails. Perfect. You'll see." Now they walked down spiral stairs. "Super perfect. Best nails on the planet. If you want nails like hers, you won't find a better place than here. I mean upstairs. Come after. I'll give you a discount."

"Discount?"

"Ten percent. One nail for free. Unless we do the toes too, then two for free. Best deal." They stopped at the front door. "I leave you here. Have a nice reading. And see you later." She patted Jenny's shoulder and scampered back to where they came from.

The squeaky door opened slowly. Jenny stepped into a room lit up with candles.

"Welcome Jenny. Please, sit down," said Svetlana, a woman in her thirties, blond braids, red lipstick, thick

Eastern European accent; she was sitting by a round table with a glowing crystal ball, hidden among the clouds of incense.

Jenny sat in front of her. "As I explained on the phone, I found your horoscope very accurate. It felt as if you knew my story already. So here I am."

"I'm really sorry for what has happened to you. He's a horrible man."

"I know. So what should I do?"

"Tarot will give us the answer," said Svetlana and pulled out a deck of cards. "Shuffle this. Thoroughly." She passed the deck to Jenny. "Give it back." Svetlana spread the cards on the table. "Pick one."

The card showed a morbid picture of a hooded skeleton on an emaciated horse with a scythe in his hand.

"Death!" Svetlana looked terrified.

"What does it mean?" A shiver went down Jenny's spine.

Svetlana gave Jenny a sharp look. After a moment of silence she asked. "What's his name?"

"Ben Owen."

"Owen?"

"Yeah. Son of the late Alexander Owen."

Svetlana had heard about this family. *Big money!* she thought. She stood up and strolled around the room. "Very interesting." *This sort of opportunity doesn't happen very often.*

Jenny's curious gaze followed the psychic. "Why?"

"Pick one more card."

Jenny couldn't decide. "Any card? I'm not sure now, so much pressure."

Svetlana stood behind Jenny. "Take your time. It's important." She put her hand on Jenny's shoulder and dug her nails a little.

Jenny finally noticed them, beauties. The nail salon manager hadn't lied: they were just perfect.

Holy Mother, please help me, Jenny prayed silently. She picked a card and passed it to Svetlana.

"The Magician," said the psychic and passed the card

back. Jenny stared at the picture of a man standing in front of a table with a sword, a pentagram and a cup; he held a candle in his hand.

"It looks like you will have to put a spell on him."

"Spell?"

"Yeah, you want revenge, right?"

"I guess so."

"A spell is your best option. The planet of authority, Saturn, is about to meet Jupiter in Aquarius next week. It opens a window of opportunity. The cards don't lie. I know a powerful witch. Next week, due to this rare astronomical event—"

"The Jupiter and Saturn thing?"

"Yeah, this one. She will be available to the public for one night only. I can give you the details of where to find her. It won't be cheap, though." She wrote an impressive amount on a piece of paper. "Do you have that?"

"I don't, but I know someone who does."

"Who?"

"His sister. And I don't think she likes him either." Jenny had met Alice a couple of times. She seemed nice but Ben hated her. She saw them arguing once. Alice threw a drink at him.

"That makes sense," said Svetlana. "The cards tell me he's a very bad person."

"I think she might be a little pissed off. Their father died and Ben inherited the company. Alice didn't get much."

"There you go! Bring her to me and you'll get your revenge. And maybe a cut too. Look at the card. The cup is made of gold. Cards never lie."

Extra cash was tempting. "I may need to call somebody."

"Do it."

Jenny dialled the number.

"Hallo," said Dean, her friend from school, now a drug dealer. He was the one who had introduced her to Ben.

"I need your help. I have to speak to Alice Owen."

#

"Wow, they're really nice," says Igor. He complements Jenny's nails.

"I agree," says the witch.

"Oh, thank you," says Jenny, stretching her hands and wiggling her fingers. Her cheeks turn a little red. *I might've misjudged them. Maybe they're not that bad*, she thinks about the hosts. *They just look weird, but one should not judge a book by its cover.*

"Beautiful. Do you like Jenny's nails?" Baba Yaga asks Alice.

"Sure," replies Alice, but she doesn't mean it. She thinks her nails are much nicer.

"I should visit this nail salon too. But I can't be bothered," says Baba Yaga. She stretches her hands and wiggles her fingers in exactly the same way Jenny just did. The witch's nails, or rather curved claws, are covered with a thick layer of dark yellow fungus and clotted blood.

"And you're the one paying for all of this, right?" The old woman gives Alice an astute look.

"I am," replies Alice.

"Money is one thing, but you know what they say, money can't bring you happiness. Do you want to make me happy?" asks the witch.

"How?" asks Alice.

"I want her nails. They're better than mine. I'm a little jealous." Baba Yaga bites her thumbnail and pulls it out. The blood gushes out of the wounded finger and covers her mouth. She spits the claw out on the table. Igor snatches it and puts it into his mouth.

"*Khrustyashchiy*," he says.

Jenny freezes in fear. *Holy Mother…*

Alice is confused. *Is this a joke?* "Do you want me to pull out her nails?"

"I want you to kill her first. Igor, pass me the knife." He takes a dagger out of the inner pocket of his jacket and puts it on the table in front of Alice. "Kill her! Help us in a sacrifice for a high price," says Baba Yaga, pointing at Jenny.

Now Alice freezes too. In shock, not fear. Everything happens so fast. She needs a moment to think.

"Hey! One, two, three, wake up." The witch snaps her fingers in front of Alice's face. A drop of blood from the still bleeding thumb lands on Alice's forehead. Now she can see it running down the right side of her nose.

"Why me?" says Jenny. "Her nails are nicer. Look! They're nicer than mine!"

Alice looks at Jenny. The knife is between them.

"You're right, darling. They are at least as nice as yours," says Igor. He turns to the witch. "Maybe we should kill them both."

Hearing this, Alice and Jenny go for the knife simultaneously. Alice is faster. Now she holds the knife close to her chest. Her hands are shaky. *Come down! You're in control now!* she says to herself.

"I'm bored. And you don't want me to get bored. Look at her. She's just a liability for you," says the witch to Alice. "She knows you are here conspiring against your brother. You can't be sure of her intentions. She may talk. Are you even good friends?"

"No, we're not," says Alice.

Jenny runs towards the door to try to unbolt it, but Igor stops her.

"Go away!" She brandishes her rosary, her face pale in terror. *Oh my God! What do I do?*

Igor erupts with laughter. "Darling, no vampires here."

"Holy Mother…" Jenny prays.

The witch says: "If you have never done it before, and I guessed you haven't, Igor may help you. Igor would you?" He grabs Jenny from the back. "I'll get rid of the body. Nobody will ever know."

"No! Alice! I beg you!" Jenny is wiggling, trying to break free from his grip.

Baba Yaga says: "Do you want your brother to run the

company? The company that should be yours!"

Alice thinks of her childhood. Ben was their parent's favourite. They adored him. Ben this and Ben that. He would get away with anything, driving drunk, losing money, being kicked out of school. When their mother died he didn't even turn up for the funeral. And the fortune is his now. She can't let this happen. She squeezes the knife and recalls when her dad took her and Ben hunting. The wounded deer was lying on the ground. "Come on, son," Dad said. "Finish it." Ben was about to pull the trigger, but Alice pulled her trigger first. Blood oozed out of the deer's cracked head. She liked it. But Dad wasn't happy. He never took her hunting again. So she killed bugs. Then small birds and mice. One cat. But she hasn't killed a human yet.

"Yes, the business should be mine," says Alice, approaching Jenny with the knife shaking in her hand.

"The first time is always difficult," says Baba Yaga.

"Alice! Please, don't do it! I won't tell anybody, I swear!" shouts Jenny, desperately.

"She'll talk, don't believe her," says Igor.

Alice stabs Jenny in the stomach. The blood comes out of the victim's mouth. Igor pushes Jenny on Alice who loses her balance and falls to the floor. Jenny falls on her, impaled on the dagger.

"You'll burn in hell," says Jenny, spitting out blood on Alice's face.

#

The same day Jenny visited Svetlana, Ricardo, the family lawyer, met "the man for special tasks", recommended by Dean.

"Can you assure me there'll be no problems?" asked Ricardo.

"We'll do it efficiently. We'll leave a syringe at the scene. It'll look like the work of some random junkies. I forgot to ask, what do you want us to do with his wallet? Do you want it back?"

"You can keep it. And everything you'll find inside too."

Ricardo slid a suitcase across the table towards the guy who opened it to inspect the contents: a substantial amount of cash.

"Great," said the guy. "We'll not be in touch."

I hope we won't, thought Ricardo.

They shook their hands and the lawyer headed towards the exit.

As soon as he left the building of the former factory on the outskirts of the city, he took a deep breath of relief. A man of his sophistication rarely ventured to such places to meet the type of people he'd just met. He lit up a cigar and looked around. The landscape was post-apocalyptic. *It's been abandoned for as long as I remember. What a shame!* A thought of buying this place and turning it into an amusement park occurred to him as he walked to his car. He pictured a rollercoaster encircling the roof. *A mirror room would be here. A couple of carousels there…* He loved the idea. *Families having fun. New workplaces.* He recalled when his dad had taken him to an amusement park. The taste of the cotton candy. The spirit of summer holidays.

"Fuck!" He stepped into a deep puddle. The mud covered his whole foot.

#

Elizabeth, the fresh widow, stood in the doorway and admired Ricardo's athletic silhouette. He was in front of the mirror, topless, about to try on a new shirt.

"Oh, how long have you been watching me?" he asked.

When he turned his naked torso to her, her knees got a little weak. Six pack with V-shaped grooves alongside the hips. He was yummy! She licked her lips and sent him a kiss.

"Do you want to dance?" he asked and played a salsa song on his phone.

"The way you move your hips, how could I say no?" She

rolled her blond hair flirtatiously.

After a couple of spins, they lay down in bed, kissing.

"I love you," whispered Elizabeth, her hand smoothing his belly.

"I love you too," replied the lawyer and kissed her neck.

"Have you taken care of the issue?"

"Yes, I have. Don't you worry about it! It'll be done soon," he replied, undoing her bra.

Her exposed breasts were truly impressive. Probably the best money she'd ever spent. They were the reason why her late husband had asked her out; he'd admitted it many times. Great investment. Hopefully the money she'd given Ricardo to "take care of the issue" would turn out to be even a better one.

#

"What happened?" asks Alice, disoriented. She is lying on the floor and the ceiling of the cottage is spinning.

"You got a little nervous and fainted. But don't worry, it's normal," replies Baba Yaga. "Igor is preparing something that will revitalise you." She grabs Alice's hand and pulls her up. Jenny's lacerated body is still lying by the door.

"Drink this. Be careful it's hot," says Igor, passing a cup of thick, brownish liquid to Alice.

She takes a sip and twists her face. "What is it?"

"Vodka with spices. Sit down, let's discuss the details. Shall we?" says Baba Yaga.

Igor cuts Jenny's abdomen and tinkers with her guts when the ladies return to the table. Alice plugs her nose with her fingers and drinks the weird liquid in one go. It really revitalises her.

"Nice, eh?" asks the witch.

"It feels good." She feels so powerful.

"I'm glad to hear this. So, when it comes to your brother, you want him to suffer before dying?" asks Baba Yaga.

"That would be good."

"What type of pain would you like?"

"I don't know, can you suggest something?"

"I've always liked electrocution. It burns the nervous system. Very unpleasant." The witch smirks.

"Electrocution then. I trust your judgement."

"And how long would you like the agony to last?"

"Thirty seconds?"

"Come on! At least one minute," says Igor, and drops Jenny's heart in front of Baba Yaga.

"We can make it one minute at no extra cost," says the witch.

"You know what? Make it two!"

"Deal!"

Igor puts Jenny's heart into a blender he's just taken off the shelf and asks Alice: "Press on, please."

"Like tomato sauce. We're not going to drink it, are we?" asks Alice.

"No," says Baba Yaga. "It's ink. Igor, paper." She dips an old-fashioned pen in Jenny's blood and writes something down.

"Are you capable of memorising four words?" asks the witch.

"I'll try."

"Do your best, if you forget there will be no refund." Baba Yaga passes her the paper. "This is a death spell. Whisper it to his ear."

Alice reads the words.

"And this will electrocute him?" asks Alice.

"Yes, it's magic," replies the witch. "Now, eat the paper."

Oh fuck, this is disgusting, thinks Alice, putting it into her mouth. Igor passes her a cup. She swallows the paper and takes a sip without checking the content.

"Bleh, what is it?" says Alice, revolted by the salty and metallic flavour of the drink.

"Your ex-friend's blood. Oh sorry, you said you weren't

friends," says Baba Yaga.

"You said we're not going to drink it!"

"I was joking." The witch cackles diabolically.

"So are we done here?" asks Alice, a little annoyed.

"Yeah," says Igor. "You can go. I'll visit you soon, with the invoice."

#

It's already morning when Alice returns to the car. It all feels like a dream. As if it never happened. Only those red stains on her clothes disagree.

Her phone vibrates. She reads the message from her family lawyer, Ricardo: *Your brother was killed.* The message was sent a couple of hours ago, but she didn't have coverage in the forest. *Ben is dead! It can't be. I went through all this shit for nothing!*

But then she realises the company is hers now. *I'm the boss!* "I'm the boss!"

This is what the will says. Doesn't it? She's never read the will.

#

Elizabeth's phone is ringing.

"It's her," she says to Ricardo.

"Answer. Be calm."

"Hallo, Alice," says Elizabeth. "So you've got our message?" *Why did I say "our"?*

"I did. What happened?"

"He was stabbed in the park. Probably random junkies. They took his wallet," says Elizabeth. *Why did I mention the wallet?*

Awkward silence.

Ricardo shows her a piece of paper with writing on it: *Tell her to come to speak to us!!!*

"Alice," says Elizabeth. "Come home. Family should be

together in a tragic moment like this."

"I'm coming now."

Elizabeth hangs up and exhales.

"You did well," says Ricardo and kisses her cheek. "When she comes, let me speak."

#

When Alice steps into the room, Elizabeth's heart speeds up. *She'll figure it out. Oh my god. We shouldn't have done this.*

Ricardo welcomes Alice with a handshake and the three of them sit down.

"I'm really so sorry, Alice," says Ricardo.

"What a tragedy," adds Elizabeth, sobbing.

Alice nods in silence.

"Ben was not married, he didn't have any children. Well, to make a long story short, the company belongs to Elizabeth now. But she agreed to give you twenty percent of the shares."

"Alice, we care about you." *Why did I say "we"? Idiot!*

"It's a good deal for you, Alice," says Ricardo.

"He's dead! My only brother!" Alice bursts into tears.

Ricardo and Elizabeth are looking at each other with their eyebrows raised. It's not the reaction they've expected.

Elizabeth approaches Alice and hugs her. "Don't cry. Everything will be OK."

"I know," replies Alice. "Sleep my…," she whispers to her stepmother's ear.

#

"…and this was the dead spell. It just looked like a stroke," says Alice to Dean. "Even the autopsy said so!"

"So why am I still alive?" he replies.

"Because I've already used it. You don't believe me, do you?"

They're in his dingy apartment. He doesn't answer her question, just looks at her, smiling mischievously. He holds a spoon with a brownish substance over the flame of a candle, heating it. It gurgles.

"What about Jenny?" he asks.

"Jenny?"

"Ben's ex-girlfriend? Wasn't she with you?"

"Ah, yeah, Jenny. I mean, she wasn't. Why did you give her my number?"

"She had some business."

"She called me but... I don't even remember what it was about. Don't give my number to anyone any more."

"I won't."

Alice rolls her sleeve.

Dean fills the syringe. He smoothes her forearm, sprinkled with dark patches. She closes her eyes with bliss when the needle enters her vein, moaning gently.

"Do you believe me?" she asks again.

"Of course, I do," says Dean, kissing her thirsty lips. He caresses her neck. "Sleep my delusional junkie."

Just a few seconds after the injection, Alice stops breathing.

He's never killed anyone before. And he'll never kill again, he promises himself. *She'd be dead within a week anyway. Someone else would do it and get paid.* He's staring at her inert face. She was a good customer and an excellent lover. She trusted him. Maybe even loved him. Tears wet his eyes.

He squeezes the body in a big suitcase and takes it to his car.

Come on, Dean! Man up! It was a good opportunity. Now you move out and start a legitimate business, he tries to console himself while driving to the abandoned factory at the outskirts of the city. Once at the place, he takes the suitcase to a building with old machinery. He puts it in the grinder and pulls the lever.

#

"Hallo," Ricardo picks up the phone.
"It's done," says Dean. "Now…"
Dean keeps talking but a stream of endorphins hitting Ricardo's nervous system prevents him from paying any attention. He's ecstatic because he knows that according to Alexander's will, with Alice "missing" and all others dead, he's the acting CEO.

He lights up a fat cigar and blows a smoke ring.

#

Ricardo's in his mansion. He's watching himself on the TV.

"If anybody knows anything, has any information that would help us find Alice, please call us," says Ricardo on the screen. "There's a reward." The phone number together with a huge reward fee are flashing below him. "Help us find Alice."

I look so good. I should be an actor, he thinks and takes a sip of the *Château Cheval Blanc 1947* he bought yesterday. *Delicious.*

On his table there's a LEGO version of the amusement park he's planning to build on the site of the abandoned factory. Small happy figurines all over the place. A tiny version of himself is between them. A lovely view. Soon it'll be a reality.

"Sorry sir," the butler says.
"Yes," he replies without paying much attention, busy placing tiny plastic Ricardo on the rollercoaster.
"There's a man downstairs. He wants to speak to you about Ms Alice."
"Tell him to go to the police. I'm busy now."
"I tried to do that, sir. But he's very insistent."
"Did he tell you his name?"
"He said his name is Igor Yaga."

THANK YOU FOR READING

Before you go… If you liked these stories, you can make a big difference in the author's career by posting a review. It doesn't have to be long.

ABOUT THE AUTHOR

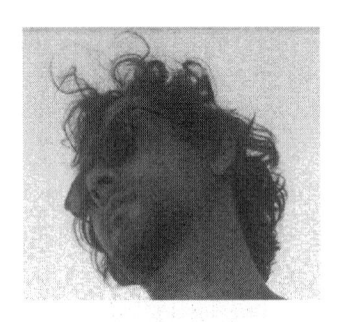

Curt Tyler is a London writer of science-fiction, horror and satire. He plays guitar and cooks good curry.

CURT TYLER Fiction

facebook.com/curttylerfiction

curttylerfiction@gmail.com

Other publications:
Extremely Rational Man and the Madness of the Law of Attraction

Printed in Great Britain
by Amazon